I Like to Read® books, created by award-winning picture book artists as well as talented newcomers, instill confidence and the joy of reading in new readers.

We want to hear every new reader say, "I like to read!"

Visit our website for flash cards, activities, and more about the series:
www.holidayhouse.com/ILiketoRead
#ILTR

This book has been officially leveled by using the F&P Text Level Gradient™ Leveling System.

Go, Go, Go!

Bob Barner

I Like to Read®

HOLIDAY HOUSE • NEW YORK

Cars go.

Trucks go.

Fire trucks go.

Buses go.

Boats go.

Bicycles go.

Stop.

Go. Go. Go.

Gone.

To young readers on the Go! Go! Go!

Library of Congress Cataloging-in-Publication Data
Names: Barner, Bob, author, illustrator.
Title: Go, go, go / Bob Barner.
Description: First edition. | New York : Holiday House, [2020] | Audience:
Ages 4–8 | Audience: Grades K–1 | Summary: A group of dogs drive a
variety of vehicles, stopping to let a flock of ducklings cross the street.
Identifiers: LCCN 2019026500 | ISBN 9780823446438 (hardcover)
Subjects: CYAC: Vehicles—Fiction. | Dogs—Fiction. | Ducks—Fiction.
Classification: LCC PZ7.B2597 Go 2020 | DDC [E]—dc23
LC record available at https://lccn.loc.gov/2019026500

ISBN 978-0-8234-4643-8 (hardcover)

ALSO BY **Bob Barner**